Maybe Someday...
ANA STORM

Copyright

Blurb

Could a love which started off selfishly become powerful enough to destroy an ancient curse? Are some lovers simply destined to become enemies? Or is it possible to build a life of happiness out of destruction?

If not now then....maybe someday.

Note: This is a short, paranormal love story, not a romance. Triggers may be present. Read at your own discretion.

Chapter 1

Juliet had always been a calm-natured person. She prided herself on possessing qualities like class, style, elegance and composure. Growing up in the elitist society in L.A, she'd taught herself at an early age how important appearances were. She was aware that engaging in any kind of...drama would only get her name plastered across the pages of a gossip magazine with the paparazzi gleefully exaggerating every action or reaction of hers. She'd learned how to behave and conduct herself gracefully as a daughter, and she had two years' worth of experience doing it as someone's wife.

She deserved a medal for the latter. It was no easy feat being married to a man such as Raiz Al' Ahmid, one of L.A's wealthiest residents. He, along with his two brothers, had been managing a successful shipping corporation as partners for almost a decade now, having started only in their college years and managing to take over the yachting game in a very brief amount of time.

Two years ago, Raiz had been considered quite a catch, and her father had believed that arranging her marriage to him would be a good business merger, packaging her off when she had barely finished her education. She hadn't protested because she loved her father, and her family had been drowning in debt. She also hadn't protested because Raiz was handsome and charismatic, and she'd admired him from afar ever since she was a teenager. She'd thought it wouldn't be so bad, being married to a rich, good-looking guy who was interested in a wife as well. She'd thought she'd be able to have a good life with him, even if they weren't in love with each other.

But as the months went by, Juliet's patience dissolved with each new spectacle she witnessed in her marriage. Raiz barely looked her way unless he wanted sex on the nights when he wasn't out cheating on her. She knew he was cheating because she'd read the dirty messages he exchanged with other girls all the time. Girls who knew her as his wife. He disrespected her by having those affairs and never even attempted to apologize whenever she broached the subject with him. He was cold, rude and arrogant beyond measure. All he cared about was his business and his women.

And it came to a point when she could no longer stand it. When she couldn't allow herself to be pushed to the sidelines and mistreated. She was a human being, not some acquisition of his. And she was fucking tired of his bullshit.

"Why don't you just file for a divorce?" a lazy voice drawled in her ear as she leaned against the metal rails of the yacht and stared daggers at her husband's back on a warm, spring evening out in the water.

Juliet swirled the wine in her glass and took a sip, trying to curb the urge to throw it into the face of the man who was speaking to her. He was no better, encouraging Raiz in his cheating ways and making it a mission almost every night to rotate himself and his brothers through all the hottest clubs in L.A, as if they were afraid that there would be some girl left unfucked.

"Oh, wait, let me guess," Tamar, Raiz's older brother continued. "The prenup, right? You're not getting a single dollar if you decide-"

"Do you want something, Tamar?" Juliet interrupted, throwing him a scathing glance.

His eyes traveled down from her face to her cleavage and lingered there. "Maybe."

Juliet sucked in a breath and without another thought, tossed the contents of the wine glass in his face. Tamar backed off a couple of steps, the liquid dribbling down his throat to stain the collar of his white shirt.

"Jesus, you didn't have to get so dramatic," he said angrily, taking out a napkin and wiping his face.

"I'm your brother's wife," Juliet hissed, clenching her fists. "Show some fucking respect."

"The hell is going on with you two?"

They both looked up at Raiz's sudden appearance while he glared at them, his large frame a silhouette against the back lights from the party he was hosting on his yacht that evening.

"Nothing, I was just leaving," Tamar muttered, walking off with long, angry strides.

Raiz watched him go before directing his attention to his wife. "Go and apologize," he ordered. "I saw you throwing your drink at him, Juliet. What is the matter with you?"

She glared back at him and opened her mouth to let him know exactly what his brother had done to deserve that treatment from her, but then she stopped herself. He didn't care. Her husband never cared. The fact that he had reprimanded her without even trying to find out the reason behind her actions only solidified his lack of interest in what went on in her life. She was supposed to stay on the sidelines and do her duty. Supposed to keep her opinions to herself and simply treat the people who were important to him with respect, whether they deserved it or not.

Taking a deep breath, Juliet responded to him with a very calm and calculated, "Fine."

And then she walked away, a new resolve settling inside her. To teach this man, her cruel husband, a big fucking lesson. An effective slap on his face before she left him for good. Her father would just have to deal with the consequences.

She found Tamar in his luxury cabin on the far end of the yacht. He was rifling through his wardrobe for a spare shirt, standing there in just his casual black slacks, his upper body exposed and if she was honest with herself, absolutely delicious. He had brown skin, just like his other two brothers, and she found herself thinking of Raiz and how, in spite of her growing hatred for him, she liked the way his hands looked on her pale body whenever they had sex. Lately, even the sex was becoming rare. And she was getting very frustrated.

If he could do it, then so could she. Men weren't the only ones with needs.

Tamar finally found another shirt and turned around, pausing when he spotted her leaning against his closed cabin door.

"Sister-in-law," he greeted her dryly. "Did Raiz send you to come and say sorry to me? There's no need. I *was* a bit of an asshole."

She narrowed her eyes at him. "A bit?"

Tamar grinned in response, his white teeth gleaming against that brown complexion. "You looked lonely. I was only trying to help."

Juliet went quiet. Tamar didn't put on the shirt, a tiny frown on his forehead an indication of curiosity. Almost a minute passed before he raised an eyebrow, detecting the hunger in her expression.

She made herself move towards him, boldly keeping her eyes on his face, and when she reached him and was only a few inches away, she licked her lips and whispered, "Look at me again. The way you looked at me out there."

He didn't seem surprised by her words and let his eyes rest on her cleavage once more. Juliet felt her body start to tingle with anticipation and desire the longer he continued to stare at her breasts. And using that rising lust as courage, she lifted her hands and slid the straps of her short dress down her shoulders, allowing it to pool on the floor.

She wore panties but no bra, and Tamar seemed to like that. He didn't hesitate, bringing his hands up to fondle her bare breasts, making her moan softly.

"Beautiful," he whispered reverently, bringing his head down to wet her nipples with his mouth. "You think I don't show you respect, Juliet? Doesn't this feel like I'm respecting you? Savoring and appreciating you? Worshiping your gorgeous body the way he never does."

She couldn't take it anymore, her arms wrapping around his strong shoulders as she pressed her heated body to his. Tamar let out a groan and walked backwards until they both fell on his bed, kissing hungrily. Juliet wasn't patient. She wanted this too much. It had started out as a means to get back at her husband, but now she physically craved it. Her pussy was wet and sensitive, her senses all foggy.

She didn't wait as she unzipped his trousers and freed his erect cock from its confines, leaning down to take it in her mouth.

"Oh, fuck, babe," her husband's brother whispered, his fingers threading through her hair. "Yes, Jesus, suck that cock for me."

She did as he asked, taking his thickness in her mouth and swirling her tongue around it, making sounds she had never even made with Raiz. She didn't care tonight. She could just let go and enjoy having sex like any normal person should do. Tamar was convenient and hot, and she was willing to indulge in this for a few minutes before she said goodbye to this world forever.

"Condom," Tamar said shortly as Juliet removed her panties and proceeded to straddle him.

"No. We don't need one," she said breathlessly, not giving a shit as she lowered herself onto her brother-in-law's cock.

Throwing her head back, she rode him hard, just taking everything she could from him. It felt amazing, being able to let go and enjoy fucking a man because she wanted to and not because she was married to him. Fuck Raiz Al' Ahmid. He could go to hell after this for all she cared. She hoped that all his boats would sink and he would become bankrupt very soon.

Juliet moaned loudly as she came all over Tamar's dick, biting her lip as satisfaction raged through her. His hands gripped her hips as she strained against him, taking every last drop of his cum. His very forbidden cum. It made her feel so dirty and empowered at the same time.

Fuck you, Raiz. Fuck you and fuck this marriage.

Chapter 2

R^aiz Sometime around midnight, my wife walked in on me screwing the girlfriend of one of my business associates in my cabin. She stood in the doorway and watched, remaining frozen on the spot as I fucked Catherine into next week. Of course by the time I actually saw Juliet, I was too far gone to stop. My orgasm was rippling through me and as it did, I locked eyes with her and found that I couldn't look away.

She wouldn't look away either, her expression containing both pain and desire as I opened my mouth slightly, shuddering and sweating from the exertion. We stared at each other for what seemed like ages but it was only for a few seconds...and then she turned around and left.

With a swallow, I fell on my back and ran a hand through my sweat-dampened hair, breathing hard. Catherine curled up next to me while I absently hooked an arm around her shoulders. My gaze went to the door again, a guilty feeling infiltrating the aftermath of my pleasure. She always made me feel that way, and I really resented her for it.

Chapter 3

It shouldn't have hurt. Watching him with someone like that. It shouldn't have hurt her, but it did. That was the first time she'd ever caught him in the act. She knew that it wasn't fair of her to react this way or feel this way when just minutes ago, she'd been on top of his brother. But fuck...

Raiz.

Why was he so cruel? Why didn't he show her at least an ounce of sensitivity or respect? This marriage meant nothing to him. It was just a facade. Something to be shown on paper. And she was the fool.

Back in her cabin, Juliet drew a bath and settled in, trying to calm her mind, but those emotions kept raging through her. Of failure and uselessness. Rejection. She wasted two years of her life on this man. There wasn't anywhere she could go now because they were in the middle of the ocean. Tomorrow, she'd be packing her bags first thing.

Juliet. How pathetic could you be? Marrying to save your family from debt. Secretly pining for a husband who couldn't give less of a shit about you. Fucking his brother and proving yourself to be just as faithless as he is. What good did it do?

Well except for that wild orgasm Tamar had given her... It had been a while.

She sighed and reclined in the tub, absently looking at the soap bubbles, feeling alone and miserable. She had no job qualifications, so she didn't know what she was going to do with herself after this. Her father would probably hate her, and she'd get no money from Raiz. She was fucked.

Her strength seemed to be leaving her along with any motivation she had had. Depressive thoughts made her sink further into the tub until her head was under water, and she could drown out every sound from the party going on up on deck. And from the cabins nearby where people were enjoying their orgies or hook-ups. In one of those cabins, her husband was busy fucking another woman.

She closed her eyes after a while, imagining herself being able to sleep half as well as he did. She hardly ever could. Sleepless nights had become a norm for her. But the water made her feel better. It really did. She was at home in it. So much that she wanted to stay inside that tub forever.

Everything faded away after a while. Her mind swirled with images of things she had never seen in her life.

Black sand on a far away coast.

An ancient-looking ship.

Pirates, sirens...

Her heart thudded faster as those images became almost kaleidoscopic. They spoke of things not separate from her existence, from who she was. And that was strange. Juliet knew for a fact that she had never been on that coast, never seen ships like that except in movies and books. The idea of pirates was laughable to her. And sirens? Even more so.

But the images persisted, making her feel things. Someone was chanting something in the background. Something about curses and doom.

Who was that siren in her dream?

Was it a dream or a nightmare? Because the creature was so hideous and terrible.

It wanted to *kill* him. It wanted to kill Raiz. No. Juliet didn't want him to get hurt. *Leave him alone, you witch!*

"Juliet?!" Someone shook her hard before gently slapping her face.

She didn't like that. She didn't appreciate the interruption because that meant that she couldn't save the man she loved from that creature. *Raiz, I don't want to lose you.*

Rage ignited deep within her until it turned into a blazing inferno. Whoever it was that had dared to pull her away from her slumber, she wanted to make them pay. She wouldn't let harm come to Raiz even in a nightmare, and she was prepared to fight against consciousness for it.

"Let me go!" Juliet shrieked at the person still shaking her and bared her teeth at him, his movements forcing her to open her eyes.

He did let go of her then and fell on his bottom, staring at her in horror.

It was Raiz. He wasn't hurt. He was right there in front of her. He'd been trying to...

"Oh my goddess," she said, wiping the water which was streaming down her face. "Did I fall asleep in the tub?"

He was still gaping at her, frozen. She blinked at him and was about to thank him for saving her life when she happened to glance down and caught sight of her lower body in the tub. This time, she was the one who froze. Shit. Her legs...

Her legs were...

What the hell was happening to her? She felt tears welling up in her eyes as she witnessed the thing which had her in shock. She didn't have her legs anymore. Her lower body was scaly and looked like a tail.

Juliet wanted to throw up. Was this a hallucination? Had she had too much wine? What? What was this?

"Raiz?" She looked back at her husband pleadingly, not knowing what to do.

That was when her eyes fell on her reflection in the mirror behind him, and a chill ran down her spine at the sight of her face. It was so grotesque. The face of the woman in her nightmare. The siren.

She felt goosebumps rising on her chilly skin, her lips wobbling with the cry which wanted to escape. At least, they looked like lips. They were thin, dark flaps, pulled back at the sides to reveal sharp teeth.

"No," she sobbed, unable to stop staring at the hideous reflection. "What is happening to me, Raiz? Please help me."

He shifted slowly, backing away from her until he had created some distance between them. With every inch he backed off, Juliet's heart broke a little more. She had thought...

When he came to save her, she had allowed herself to believe for a moment that there was a part of him which cared about her. But his reaction now told her otherwise. He looked scared. And disgusted by her.

"Raya," he whispered, shaking his head as he got to his feet.

They stared at each other and there was something in his eyes, a knowledge and awareness which she had never seen before. Like he had discovered some secret which she was oblivious to.

"Please," she cried, tears running down her cheeks in helplessness. She couldn't look at herself anymore. She wanted to die.

What was wrong with her?

"It was you all this time," he said, again with a whisper. "It was you. I thought I'd escaped all of that. I thought I could live this life without being cursed. I didn't make anyone fall for me. Didn't make any fake promises. Then why? Why can't you just let me live?!"

Now she was starting to believe that he was losing his mind as well. What was he talking about? She had no idea what any of it meant. But there was one thing he said which her soul protested against so strongly, and she had to say something to correct him.

"I did fall in love with you, Raiz," she confessed in a trembling voice. "I didn't want to admit it because of the way you treated me. How humiliating it was for me to admit that I could love a man who thought nothing of me. Had no respect for our marriage. But I did fall for you. I love you so much."

He swallowed hard at her admission, suddenly turning to thump his fist into the open door of their cabin. "No, damn it!" he growled, sounding pained. "You can't love me, Juliet. You can't. It will end in my death. Don't you understand? Don't you remember anything?"

The pain in his voice cut at her soul. She couldn't bear to see him like that. It was so strange because an hour ago, she would have given anything to make him feel this way about her. To torture him and punish him. But now she just wanted to protect him. Whatever this curse was, he seemed to believe in it so strongly. He sounded genuinely afraid. And she had never known Raiz Al' Ahmid to be afraid.

"I will never hurt you," she said softly, trying to push her self-loathing and fear regarding her predicament aside to console him. "Raiz, I don't care that you can't love me the same way. I'll leave tomorrow. You can be free of me. Please don't be afraid. I'm just... I'm confused. I don't know what to do about all of this. What is going on?"

He didn't turn to look at me. He just stared at the door for a moment before muttering, "Get out of the water. You will be all right. Get dressed and warm up. And please for fuck's sake, do not sing."

What the...?

He was gone before she had a chance to respond.

...

Chapter 4

The Heretics had been around in Ayran for hundreds of years, known for their strength, resourcefulness and dark magic. The Puritans had always been warned to stay away from them. To not mix around with the native tribe members. They were only good as laborers. They needed money and the Puritans needed their services. That was as far as their interactions went. Raya had grown up in that small seaside village and not once in her life had she ever had more than a ten-second interaction with any of them.

Her brother made sure of that. After the death of their parents during a shipwreck, her thirty year old brother, who had been a young boy back then, had inherited the shipping business. Now he ran it as ruthlessly as he ran his household, making sure that young Raya never stepped out of line. It was stifling. Thomas was responsible, not cruel to her. But he wasn't very affectionate either. Raya yearned to be able to feel that kind of affection from someone. She was almost nineteen years old, and soon, her brother was going to marry her off. To some boring old merchant. A merger which would benefit his business as well as get her off his hands.

She was panicking. She couldn't marry anyone. Because she was already in love. With a man she had never even spoken to.

His name was Raiz. And he was a Heretic. Completely forbidden to her. Maybe that was part of his allure. Or maybe it was just every single thing about him which fascinated her endlessly. His dark hair and brown skin, his sharp eyes, strong physique and that rare, rambunctious laughter. The way he frowned so deeply when he got mad at something and his beautiful mouth pinched together to express his displeasure. Raya didn't care what her people said about his kind. She thought he was incredible. His tribe members, from what she had observed, were pretty big on maintaining a strict code of honor. None of them had ever touched anyone from her sect. They kept to themselves, worked hard and enjoyed their solidarity. She envied them sometimes. Especially the bond Raiz had with his friends, Kal and Tamar, and other tribe members. The way he doted on his little sister, Kaelyn.

Her existence was so lonely that she would gladly marry him and become one of the 'outcasts' just to be in that kind of space. They all seemed so happy together. Content with their lot. Not greedy or mercenary.

But it was an impossible dream. Raiz hardly even looked her way. Marrying him was out of the question.

Chapter 5

R^{aiz} "Let me take your coat, brother. Do you want to have dinner now or later?"

"Kaelyn, you know you do not have to do this. I can hang my own coat and serve myself dinner."

My sister stepped back to give me a wry look. "I know. But taking care of you is the only way I feel better about not being able to contribute towards-"

"Stop." I shot her a frown, knowing exactly what she had been about to say. "How many times have we talked about this? You do not need to contribute anything. You're my younger sister. It is my responsibility to take care of you. Provide for you. And then find you a nice husband-"

"You were being so sweet until you said the word 'husband,'" she huffed before turning away. "I don't want to get married."

"Okay," I said in a gentler tone and placed a hand on her shoulder. "You don't have to if you don't want to. I like having you around. You know that."

"I prepared your bath," she quipped.

I let out a sigh. "Kaelyn."

"Just go freshen up, and I'll serve dinner."

It was pointless arguing with her. She was in the mood to play caretaker this evening. And to be honest, I was pretty tired. Work had been exhausting today at the docks. I decided to let it be and allow her to do whatever made her feel better. She was so fucking sweet, I didn't know what to do with her sometimes. No matter what she said, I knew that she needed to marry soon. It was just our way. A few of the young men in our tribe had shown interest, but nobody seemed perfect enough for my little princess. I had to think this through carefully. Find her a man who would treat her the way I have treated her all these years ever since the death of our parents. Kaelyn was that one bright spark in my life, and I needed her to shine forever, so that I would have a reason to keep going. Because some days, everything in life seemed pointless.

I was paid such crappy wages, I could hardly afford even the minimal of comforts on my income. I tried not to let Kaelyn know how much that bothered me, but she was pretty intuitive and managed to catch on to my stress. Last night, she'd tried to question me, but I avoided her queries by rushing out to meet my friends. They were no better off than me, having families to feed and making do with whatever they were paid.

Even though I was tired, I still went out after dinner that night to keep my friends company. Kaelyn wanted to stay home and read, so I let her. Every evening, our tribe had a gathering out on the beach, unless the weather was too rough and windy. That didn't stop all of us though. We Heretics were savages, always had been. We were coastal creatures and our lineage was centuries old. A little thing like bad weather did not stop us from enjoying ourselves.

"You took a bloody long time, princess," my friend, Kal, greeted me from beside the bonfire, tipping his bottle of moonshine at me. "I thought you'd bail on us tonight."

I grabbed the bottle out of his hands, taking a nice, long sip of the burning liquid before wiping my mouth off on my sleeve. "Me? Bail on my brothers? Never." I looked around the crowded beach for Tamar and turned back to Kal when I could not locate him.

He smirked at me and jerked his chin towards the darkened caves at the bottom of the cliff wall beside us. "He needed to get warm," Kal shared.

With a snort, I sat down next to him on the rock, staring into the fire and sharing the moonshine with him as we waited for Tamar to finish his business and get back.

"He gets really lucky with the girls," I commented after it felt like the silence between us had stretched out for too long.

Kal grunted and replied, "You would too if you stopped being so picky. I'm sure you've noticed the way they all stare at you, Raiz. And I don't just mean from our tribe."

His words made me swallow a huge gulp of moonshine and then start to splutter because it went down the wrong way, burning my nostrils and making my eyes tear up.

"I'm fine," I growled at him when he tried to make sure that I was okay.

Why did he have to mention that to me right now? The 'not just from our tribe' part. It brought *her* to mind. The girl I shouldn't be thinking about. The Puritan. My boss' little sister.

Not so little, anymore, Raiz. Have you noticed the way she's filled out? Those breasts...

"No, fuck, no!" I snapped, and Kal gave me a stunned look.

"Raiz, calm down. I didn't mean to piss you off."

I shook my head in frustration and added, "It's not you. It's her," I spat out. "She keeps staring at me. Hell, I can't even work in peace some days. Those 'come fuck me' looks she gives me. Does she not know who I am? What I am."

Kal began to snicker which angered me even more.

"What's so funny?" I snapped again.

He grinned widely, his face lit up by the dancing firelight. "She knows, my friend. It's common knowledge. She just wants that supernatural cock."

I scoffed and looked away, but inside my pants, my 'supernatural' cock stirred at the prospect of being inside her, taking that Puritan virginity of hers and giving her a taste of my Heretic cum. It was what she longed for so much. I should just use her to get rid of this ache she was responsible for creating in me in the first place and then cast her aside once I was done.

"It's a sin," I muttered to no one in particular. "A sacrilege. We are forbidden to mate with Puritans. It could result in our whole tribe being exiled from Ayran. I will not be responsible for that."

"It's just sex," Kal replied casually.

Kal was always the casual one out of us three. The one who refused to live life based on tradition and superstitions. But I was willing to bet that even he had not broken this centuries-old sacred rule regarding coupling between a Heretic and a Puritan. It had something to do with a bitter feud between our ancestors and a vile curse being unleashed. We were told our people had the kind of dark, corrupt magic which was an abhorrence to Puritans. And that was why we had been cast aside. Any intimate associations between us was forbidden. And it needed to stay that way. I was not willing to test the powers that be just for a couple of fucks with someone like Raya.

Raya.

Even her name did things to me which I hated to describe. I was nineteen and very much ready to be with a woman in the physical sense. But like Kal had said, I was too picky. I didn't like being in close contact with anyone much. But it was time I did pick someone. And relieved my frustrations through her instead of entertaining thoughts about the enemy.

I made myself think about other stuff, but that was when Kal happened to mutter, "You know she is the key to Thomas' fortune right now. She is the only way to get to his stash. We've been dealing with these miserly wages for years, Raiz. We deserve better. We deserve to be paid for what we are worth. And if we can't get it fairly, there's only one other way."

I frowned as I took in his meaning, squinting into the flames in front of me and feeling my heart race at the thought of taking what was owed to us from right under Thomas' nose. Stealing. I felt excited by it even though I had never seriously considered it before.

But he was right. We were paid very poorly while they lived like kings. It was not fair at all. Ayran was as much ours as it was theirs. So why all this segregation? Why wasn't a Heretic allowed to be rich here? To open up a decent business. To have shares in a shipping business?

These archaic laws should no longer apply. We had more than proved that we could be peaceful, not savages like those fuckers believed. And we were hardworking as well.

"If I were you, my brother, I would take that 'come fuck me' invitation and make the most of it. Drill her while drilling all the information out of her as well. Like where her brother hides all the treasure he hoards. Take one for the team, why don't you? Be your people's hero. Destroy that motherfucker and make us all rich. Give us back our power since accessing our magic is out of the question."

Legend said that long ago, a devout Puritan, against whom one of our oldest ancestors had used his dark magic, had prayed to the gods and had him cursed. Had our entire lineage cursed. So we would forget how to tap into our magic no matter how much we tried. We would feel it in our blood, in our bones, but never be able to use it. And it would torture us a little to feel that frustration. Every Heretic to come was cursed like this. And nobody knew the cure.

I wasn't sure if that was true or not. I hardly felt anything in my blood or bones. Most of the time, I just felt dead inside.

But I could make myself useful now that I was old enough. Try to help my people, my tribe. Kaelyn would be better off if I could somehow acquire more wealth for us. I sighed to myself and tossed back some more moonshine, this time, not diverting my thoughts when the image of Raya in a loose, flimsy little dress flashed across my mind. I fixated on that image and got drunk on the liquid burning down my throat, warming my chest and stomach.

I guess it wouldn't kill me. To take one for the team. I was thinking of the greater good. I didn't really give a fuck about her.

Chapter 6

She was searching for an old copy of a novel she used to read as a child. It was hard to recall the name of it. She held the candle to the shelf in front of her and peered at the dusty volumes lining it in the library at the back of the house. It was almost midnight; everything was silent and a little spooky here because the servants were out and her brother was asleep upstairs. But she could not find rest, so she decided to read something which brought her comfort.

When she felt a pair of arms go around her and a hard, warm body press into her from behind, she stifled a gasp. The scent of sea flooded her nostrils, followed by a musky male essence which mingled with the aroma of rosemary and crystal candles burning in mason jars in the library. It was heady and exciting, having him come up and catch her unawares like that, like he had been doing for the past couple of nights. But it was also pretty risky.

"You can't be here," Raya whispered frantically, gasping when his arms tightened deliciously across her bodice, crushing her breasts and making them almost pop out of her nightie.

A hot, curling ache of desire ran along her body at this contact, and all she wanted to do was melt in his arms and let him ravish her right there against the bookshelves.

"I'm running out of patience, my love," he drawled seductively, trailing his nose along her jawline, his silky hair tickling her neck. "My need for you is getting so strong, so intense and powerful. Raya, I can't sleep without you at nights. My body craves yours. It wants to be one with you."

"Oh, goddess," she gasped again, starting to breathe faster at his heated confessions, his proximity and ardor.

Liquid heat was forming at her center and she needed him to take care of it so bad. Just like she instinctively knew he wanted her to take care of that hard length pressing against her bottom.

"Raiz, my brother could catch us. You need to leave."

"Fine."

His tone was cold all of a sudden. Dismissive. And she hated that. When he withdrew from her and turned away, Raya desperately reached out to clutch at his shirt collar to stop him from leaving. The movement of his powerful shoulder under her palm was all she felt before her senses exploded as he twisted to crush her back against the bookshelves, making her candle fall to the floor and snuff out. A muffled sound escaped her when Raiz lifted her until she had her thighs wrapped around his hips, her night dress disheveled, revealing creamy skin which he explored possessively.

Her arms were tight around his neck, her tongue caught up in a passionate rhythm with his as he kissed her hard, grinding his heated length along her already moist core. She wanted that thing in her. She really did. But not this way.

"Raiz...please...we can't..."

She could no longer protest when his rough hands fondled her breasts, his face lowering to push between them and rub, a wet sensation telling her that he had his tongue out and was sweeping it across her nipple. Raya moaned helplessly this time. Vaguely, she heard someone calling her name before she was lowered abruptly to the floor and found herself alone in the space of a few seconds.

"Raiz?" she whispered in the semi-darkness of the shelves. "Raiz? Where are you?"

She moved forward and stumbled into someone, almost letting out a scream, but it was only Thomas.

"Raya, what are you doing?" her brother questioned harshly, shining a candle in her face.

She turned her back to him and quickly straightened her dress, lest he see the blush of desire on her pale skin, her lips which probably had smudged rogue on them and the telltale sign of hard nipples.

"I was just looking for some books," she mumbled, folding her arms across her stomach, already missing her lover...who was not yet a lover in the physical sense.

"In the middle of the night? Raya, go back to sleep. This addiction of yours is starting to worry me. You should be thinking about your marriage."

With that dismissal, her brother stumbled away, leaving a lone candle next to her on the shelf. He never understood her love of books and literature. Her thirst for knowledge. He considered it a useless interest. It saddened her that her only value in his eyes was how marriageable she was.

Overwhelmed by the awful monotony and hopelessness of her existence, she turned back to the shelf and leaned her forehead against the sweet, cedar wood. She was falling more and more in love with Raiz Al' Ahmid with each passing day. And he never once spoke of a future with her. She needed to swallow her pride and ask. Ask the man just what it was he wanted from her. Because she could not go on like this anymore.

It didn't matter if it was forbidden for a Heretic and a Puritan to unite in love and intimacy. She couldn't imagine her life without him and was willing to battle the gods and all their curses to have a future with him.

Chapter 7

Raiz

I was overpowered by the kind of lust I'd never felt before in my life. Why was I even holding back? Sure, my intention had only been to gain her trust and infiltrate the secrets of her brother's shipping business. But the temptation of her luscious body, eager, soft, a combination of pearl white and pink, was too much to resist.

I'd been toying with her sexually for several days and nights, determined to get what I needed and exit her life without giving in to my needs. But tonight...I wasn't sure I'd be able to control myself. Tonight, I'd foolishly invited her on board one of the merchant shipping vessels I worked on and looked after. The boat belonged to a Puritan noble, and I had no right to use it the way I wanted to, but if everything went according to plan, I could succeed in my mission by tomorrow night.

I lit a lone candle in the cabin section of the boat, which was hidden away towards the far end of the jetty. Even over the lapping of the water on the sides of the boat, I could pick up on her footsteps. I went out quietly to greet her, taking hold of her hand which peeked out of her hooded cloak and inviting her on board.

"I thought you wouldn't come," I said as we headed inside the cabin, and I quickly locked the door behind her to keep out the chill. And for privacy, of course.

In case one of my adventurous buddies decided to come looking for me and ruined my plans.

Raya lowered the hood of her cloak and her eyes darted around the cabin, taking everything in.

"I almost got caught by the maid, but I managed to slip through later." She finally brought her gaze to me, and I was caught by surprise when she moved in and started to kiss me hungrily. "Raiz, I missed you so much."

What? I just saw her last night.

But I didn't scoff out the thought like I probably would have if my cock hadn't started to twitch at the feel of her body against mine, those curves enticing me even through the heavy cloak. Her eager lips. Her sighs and moans. Fuck. She was delicious, and I was done trying to pretend that I didn't want to take a dip inside her wetness and slide my hard cock in and out of her.

"Do you want to marry me, Raiz?" she whispered as her soft mouth glided over my jaw and her hands traveled up the front of my shirt, tangling in the sparse hair on my chest after opening the first couple of buttons.

"Of course," I found myself murmuring as those hands dipped further down and touched my nipples and abdomen. Wow. She was feisty this evening. So bold and forward.

"I can't stop thinking about you," she whined suddenly, stepping back to let her cloak slide off, all the while keeping her eyes on me. "I felt so bad last night when you had to leave...when we couldn't...um...make love."

I blinked at the term she used. Make love? What the hell did that mean? And then I knew exactly what she meant when she finally undressed, and I saw that she was completely naked under the cloak.

Gods. Look at that perfection. My cock was straining at the seam of my pants now.

She was so perfectly shaped. Her skin appeared silky and glowed a little from the flickering light of the candle. Her breasts, which had been enchanting me more than anything else lately, swung free and were pink-tipped, her nipples pebbled. My mouth began to water at the sight of it all, and suddenly, the raging lust in me was out of control.

I whipped off my shirt and reached out to haul her into my arms, letting out a groan as her body collided with mine, so much softness meshing with my calluses and strength.

"Give me these," I growled, bending my head to her tits and noisily sucking on one tasty nipple.

Raya moaned and threw her head back, cradling my head in her hands as she allowed me to lick, suck, kiss and grope her beautiful breasts.

My cock was hard and impatient. I moved us further inside the cabin and lifted her to plant her ass on one of the tables in the corner, pushing the rest of the items on it to the floor.

"Open your legs for me, Raya," I growled again, massaging my erection through my pants and squinting at her. "Let me see that pretty pussy of yours."

Raya gasped slightly at my command, but she seemed too far gone with lust for me as well because she leaned back on her elbows and propped her heels on the edge of the table, parting her thighs and showing me the pink, glistening core of her which would soon be mine to take.

Fuck. She was so wet. I knew a woman needed to be wet in order to accommodate an erect penis, so this would go better than I had anticipated.

Taking two fingers, I instinctively slid them over her pussy, parting her folds slowly. Raya moaned at the contact and her thighs lay open even more, inviting me to do what I needed to do so badly. I didn't hesitate. I took my cock out and grazed the tip of it along her lips, sucking my breath in through my teeth at the pleasure. Raya let out another sensual sound and closed her eyes, her breasts pointing up at me, head thrown back in abandon.

And then I pushed forward, thrusting hard inside her, ignoring her sharp cry and the slight barrier I encountered. I didn't fucking care about any of it. I selfishly just wanted to rut in her and spill myself inside that warm, wet cunt.

Grunting with my thrusts, grabbing her thighs and finding a rough rhythm, I barely even looked at her face as I continued. This physical ecstasy was unlike anything I'd ever experienced. I was lost in the moment, breathing hard and letting my hips drive forward instinctively. Fuck. The hell had I been missing out on all this time? No wonder Tamar was always disappearing off after work, trying to get under whatever skirt he could find for the evening. A man could get addicted to this sort of thing. I wished she could be my whore forever, ready and waiting for me whenever I wanted to do this, but after a couple of nights, I would have no more use for her.

She would always be the enemy. The Puritan. I had no interest in being with her in any way. The fucking was just something I hadn't been able to help. Far off in the night, I heard a rumble of thunder. The hair at the back of my neck seemed to stand as a whisper of wind curled around my bare back. The lone candle flickered and suddenly, the flame was snuffed, but there was no wind. I couldn't figure out that mystery though because I was too busy pumping my cock inside the sweet, greedy cunt of this Puritan, which she so stupidly offered me.

"Take it," I ordered her roughly when she said my name in the dark. "Take my cock. Take all of it. Gods."

"Raiz, please, you... Say you love me," her pleading voice sounded through the haze of my lust.

I wanted to laugh at her, but I was coming so hard, and all I could manage was a deep growl as my seed shot inside her. What an incredible feeling this was. Too bad I found it between the legs of someone I could hardly stand to be around. I needed to find myself a nice girl from my tribe because now that I'd had this sort of pleasure, I didn't think I could stay without it.

"Fuck," I breathed out as the last few drops of my cum drained out of my still pulsing cock.

I tried not to collapse on top of her even as my knees went a little weak. Steadying myself against the edge of the table, I gathered my breaths before pulling out of her and stepping back. I could hardly see anything in the dark. It was probably good. I didn't want to see her, anyway. I was feeling a little tired and just wanted to go home and rest.

"Come on," I took her hand and pulled her to her feet, cursing as she stumbled. "You should get home before anyone starts looking for you. Here." I picked up her cloak which I felt with my boot and hastily wrapped it around her.

"Raiz, what're you-?"

"I don't have time to talk to you, Raya," I snapped at her, already dragging her to the door and not caring if she stumbled again. "This was so fucking risky. I don't know what I was thinking asking you to come here tonight. And then you pulling that kind of stunt. Fuck, what was I supposed to do?"

"Why are you behaving like this?" she cried, snatching her hand out of mine. "We just... Raiz, do you know what that meant to me? Giving myself to you like that? You are so insensitive. Is this how you show your love for me?"

I let out a heavy breath and walked out of the dark cabin, blinking a little at the bite of cold wind and some lanterns along the jetty, snapping me back to my senses. Back to reality. Shit. I'd made a mess of this. She was agitating me, and I wanted to get rid of her without drama. I was starting to get a headache. And I never got headaches. Women.

"I will speak to you tomorrow," I told her resolutely. "Wait for me at the library."

Raya let out a scoff. "I won't! I fucking won't wait for you! I hate you! Don't ever come near me again," she finished with a sob, before pushing past me and running off towards the jetty.

I frowned at her disappearing figure, feeling nothing at all for her. But the way she'd felt around my cock...that was something I wouldn't easily forget. That clench and feel of her pussy. Maybe just one more indulgence before I ruined her for good. It wouldn't be hard. She was so easy to manipulate.

28 ANA STORM

Chapter 8

She really was the most foolish girl in the whole world. Because even after telling herself that she would hate him forever, and that he was no good for her, she still waited for him at the library the next night. And she let him fuck her again, mercilessly and hard against the bookshelves.

Not once. But twice. She enjoyed it when she let herself forget how he was supposed to be treating her. She enjoyed the physical act of it so much. He was really...thorough. Raw and passionate. A bit lewd as well, but she didn't care. It felt good when Raiz was inside her. When he was hers for those few precious moments. His roughness started to appeal to her. She told herself that that was just how he was, but he had love in his heart for her. He simply needed to realize that. It would be better once they got married.

"Yes. Whatever you want, Raya," he grunted the next night as he prepared to take her in her brother's office, claiming to be feeling adventurous.

His response was in answer to her question about whether he was going to marry her soon. She wouldn't let him undress her until he agreed. And once she had his agreement, she let go of her bodice and Raiz ripped it open with his calloused, brown hands and let her breasts spill out. Goddess, why did she like this so much? It was insane.

Even as she worried about that, she hooked her legs around his lean hips and moaned hard as he fucked her raw on top of the table, watching her breasts bouncing with each thrust of his. She felt so naughty and full of lust, closing her eyes and starting to give it back to him the same way he was giving it to her. Fuck. The sounds they made together. Her brother could walk in any minute and catch them. But she wanted that crudity for some reason. She wanted him to be that way with her and make her feel...dirty. She was tired of being a Puritan all the time.

Once, before he began fucking her, he actually slapped her there. Hard. And she gasped, not because it stung...but because it made her core even wetter and made her crazier. What was wrong with her? Why couldn't she stop? All day long, she just dreamed of him coming to her at night so that his cock could bury itself deep inside her. Over and over.

"Raiz, I love you. I love you so much," she whispered in his ear the next night as he pounded into her.

"Yes. I know. I love you too. Fucking give it to me. Gods, you're so wet," he replied, making her melt into a puddle of affection and raging desire.

"Have you noticed that every single time we make love, thunder rolls across the sky and candles get snuffed out?" she giggled as she lay naked and sweaty in her bed with him hours later.

"Yes. I think we both anger and embarrass the gods," he said lightly.

Raya giggled again and draped herself over him, kissing his jaw. She loved his smell, salty like the ocean, a little sweaty and a little bit like incense although she had no idea how that came about. "I love you so much. Raiz, I was thinking-"

"I have to be at the docks very early," he interrupted as he moved away. "It's a sunrise shift. See you tomorrow night."

She barely made out his figure in the dark as he got out of bed and dressed. Part of it was due to the darkness. Part was due to the glassiness of her gaze as tears sprang up in her eyes. She wanted to ask him to stay. She wanted him to chase away that feeling of wrongness. Of doom. To tell her that he really wanted to marry her. But she remained silent, her throat feeling tight with pain as he left her bedroom.

Young men, she had been told by her maid, *were fickle sometimes. Scared of settling down. It was better not to push them.* And Raiz was only nineteen. She didn't want him to feel suffocated or pressured by her demands. But her period was late and she was very worried about the future.

She believed that he did love her a lot even if he was wary of commitment. If she spoke to him calmly and told him her fears, he might listen. Tomorrow night, she needed to get her brain off his cock, and talk about important stuff. Like their future together.

...

7 moons.
7 moons will pass before the curse takes effect.
Do not tread the water.
Do not approach the sand.
Keep away, Puritan.
Or else you will be doomed.
And you will become his doom as well.
The bastard of the ocean. The Heretic.

SHE WOKE UP GASPING and sweaty, clawing at her neck as the need for water overpowered her. Her throat itched so bad, and her heart was pounding. What had that dream been all about? Who had that sinister voice belonged to? It sounded so familiar. Raya's body was stiff with fear and legs heavy as lead. But she needed water, so she made herself move, feeling around on her nightstand for the pitcher and not bothering to pour the liquid in a glass. She just gulped it down like that, streams of it falling on the front of her open robe.

She'd slept only in her robe that night, laying herself bare for her lover who had a habit of sneaking up on her and always surprising her with his readiness to get inside of her body. Raya didn't mind that anymore. She wanted that. It thrilled her so much.

But this time, Raiz hadn't come to her. Her bed was empty. And her heart felt so cold. Once she had quenched her thirst, she let out a sigh and tried to forget that horrible dream. A nightmare where she had been unable to breathe and someone had been warning her to stay away from the coast. And what did the dream figure mean with her becoming Raiz's doom? She could never. She would never hurt him. She'd rather die. Raiz meant everything to her. She'd find out if he was okay tomorrow. She refused to think that her daring and passionate lover had been harmed in some way. That dream was stupid. Superstition roamed so freely in the heads of the people of Ayran, even hers. She had to learn to separate myth from reality.

Chapter 9

Raiz

I came home one night to discover my sister...my sweet Kaelyn...hanging from the ceiling of our living room. I was paralyzed with shock at first, watching in horror as my friends, my brothers, Tamar and Kal, rushed in from behind me and lowered her limp body to the ground. I wept so hard that night, lashing out at the other two when they tried to console me, tried to help.

No. She was my sister. I was going to bury her all by myself. And so I did. Out in the rain in our tribal graveyard, digging a hole in the ground for her when I'd had all these dreams of seeing her wed and happy with a husband and children.

I came back all muddy and broken after her burial to find a letter on the table.

Forgive me, Raiz. I couldn't be a burden on you anymore.

My heart tore apart at those words. When had I ever made her feel that? When? How could she have done something like this? Ended her life. And mine too. For how could I go on living when she was gone...taken from me so cruelly by this twist of fate? Kaelyn. I would have taken care of you forever. Was it because I kept talking about marrying her off? Was it my fault?

I grieved for her for two whole nights just locked up in my home, and when Raya came to see me on the third night, I couldn't fucking stand the sight of her. She was screaming at me to let her in, and finally I did, dragging her to my living room and pushing her face first into my sofa before fucking her brains out like a savage.

She kept screaming at me to stop, but I didn't want to. I wanted to punish her. For taking up so much of my attention. If I hadn't been busy satisfying this raging sexual need in me like I was possessed by a demon, I would have paid more attention to my sister. Maybe she had started to feel neglected by me. Maybe she thought I'd be better off and settle down if I wasn't taking care of her. Fuck!

I pummeled into her hard as my frustration and anger soared, and finally, when she lay limp and sobbing, I stepped away and told her to fuck off. Fucking bitch. I hated her so much. I had all the secrets I needed from her brother's office. I'd been going straight there from her bedroom for a number of nights now and stealing all the information while she slept off the exhaustion. I didn't need her anymore.

"Raiz...what is the matter with you? I just wanted to talk." She sat up and looked at me with tear streaks on her face. "I might be with child. Please. Please, just talk to me, my love. Whatever it is that you're going through, we will work it out together. I'll be here for you if you just-"

"I know a midwife," I interrupted her harshly and walked over to the kitchen to grab some money out of the jar I kept there. "Two houses down this street. Tell her I sent you. Ask no questions. Here." I threw a wad of bills at her. Money I'd been saving for Kaelyn's wedding. Now it would go towards the destruction of whatever Raya sensed was growing in her womb. Something I did not want. And certainly not with her.

Raya stared down at the money on her lap and then back up at me speechlessly. I had no patience for her right now. I'd miss the fucking, but that was it. I wanted her out of my life. There were other girls around to please me.

"Go. I never loved you, stupid girl. I just wanted to fuck. Are you really that naive? Can't you tell when a guy just wants to bed you and not fucking spend every single day wanting to look at you or dream about marrying you? How vain are you, really? Get out of my house."

Raya didn't move. She was staring at me like I was a monster, and maybe I was. Because I barely waited a minute before I got sick of her and grabbed her by the arm, forcing her out of my home and into the night before shutting the door on her face. I ignored her screams. Fuck, she was making such a scene while I was heartbroken and angry over the loss I had suffered. It only solidified my decision to end things with her.

"I should have known you'd turn out to be everything they warned us about, you fucking bastard!" Raya raged from outside and banged on my door. "I hope my nightmare comes true! I hope I really do become your doom, Raiz Al' Ahmid. You will suffer just like you are making me suffer and be destroyed just like you destroyed me today. I hate you, and I curse you a million times over!"

Thunder rolled overheard as she finished her rant, and I was startled when the candles burning inside my house snuffed out. I stared into the darkness, listening to the loud crash of waves on the beach nearby. And no Raya. Had she left already? There was nothing but silence outside my door now. I didn't want to take the risk to check if she was still there waiting to pounce on me or not, so I just stumbled off towards my room and went straight to bed.

Tomorrow, I needed to steal my treasure from Thomas and leave Ayran for good after helping out some of the poor families. I had no future here after losing the only person I had ever loved.

Chapter 10

The Heretic

Endless nights at sea meant endless amounts of reflection. Sometimes unwanted. Un-fucking-welcome. But it couldn't be helped. These thoughts would never leave me alone. Never. I barely paid attention to the moon high up in the sky, casting its beam across the black waters surrounding my ship. I had a ship now. He was called 'Bastard of the Ocean'. It was very much not a 'she' because I had grown to hate anything female now.

My existence had become so bleak...everything was fucking ruined...all because I had been stupid enough to get involved with a female.

We were several miles off the Barbary coast one day when we heard it. A song so enticing and haunting that it was hard to concentrate on anything else. It rose above the sounds of the ocean and the glide of the ship through the choppy waters. Above the sound of the wind circling around us so strongly. Above the cries of seagulls. How was that even possible? The sweet, pleading melody of her voice...so soft and vulnerable...so fucking sad.

I didn't even remember turning towards the direction of that voice, steering my ship towards an island which seemed to have appeared out of nowhere. A small cave-like structure surrounded by jagged rocks where wild waves crashed on the shore. It was blanketed with greyish fog and seemed like an ominous spot for any girl to be stranded on. What was she doing there? Why did she sound so sad and lonely? And why did I feel like going to her and taking that sadness away as soon as possible, however I could?

"Sirens," I heard someone mutter from beside me. "Gods, Raiz, what are you doing? Turn the ship around."

It was Kal. He was out of his mind if he thought I was going to turn around now. She needed me. She was calling to me. I had to reach her.

"Get the fuck out of my way," I growled as I pushed Kal aside. He'd been trying to grab the helm from me, forcing me to steer away from her. I couldn't do that. Didn't he understand? Didn't he hear the melancholy in her tone? How could I ignore that?

"Raiz, we cannot go there! Look at those rocks. The ship will be ruined, you idiot!"

Then so be it. I didn't care if the ship was going to crash on those goddamned rocks. I didn't fucking care about anything right now except getting to her.

"Tamar, stop him!" my friend yelled but the song she sang was louder in my head.

It was making my heart bleed. I'd never felt this way before in my life. I wanted to cry and lose myself in her melody at the same time. I wanted to die for her. Anything...anything to take away her sorrow.

The waves became more tumultuous as I neared the shore. Neared my destruction. But also...my salvation.

"Raiz! Turn the ship around!"

I was going to kill him if he tried to stand in my way. I really was. My hand closed around the handle of my dagger as I scowled at the shore, trying to catch a glimpse of her. And then...through the clearing fog in my line of vision, I spotted her.

My heart gave a thud at the sight of her draped over a rock; long, red hair wet and clinging to a body which made desire soar inside mine until all I could think of was taking her, right there on that shoreline, as the waves crashed around us and the cold beach became our mating ground. I was hard...so hard. And agonized because I couldn't touch her fast enough. My heartbeats began to race as my ship veered towards her. I was afraid I might hurt her, so I swung the helm away at the last minute.

Wind rushed in my ear along with her song, and I knew I was going to crash badly. The only clear path in the reef was directly between me and her. Everywhere else was rocky. But I couldn't hurt her. It didn't matter if the harm came to me and my friends. I had to protect her at all costs.

Gods, she was so alluring. So damn...

A thunderous sound erupted around me, and my body jerked hard as I was flung away from the helm, losing my balance. I heard shouts, but it barely registered in my brain as I hit my head on the side of the ship, hissing in pain.

Come to me, my love...

Even as I blacked out, I heard her calling to me. Even as the cold onslaught of water splashed over me, sucking me into its murky depths a while later, I kept hearing her voice. And my last dying wish was that I could have spent just one moment staring into her eyes, feeling her arms around me, her lips on my skin. I didn't want to lose her so soon...

Chapter 11

The siren

    She stared at her enemy's face for a long time as he lay on the beach, wet and unconscious. He was as handsome as he had always been to her. That was the first thing she noticed. The second thing was his body. Big and brown, his tattered white shirt plastered to his torso...and those black breeches clinging to his powerful legs. The bulge in front was prominent. It grabbed her attention immediately.

For months, she had been training her voice, honing her magic until she could send out her siren's call to him. The call of doom and destruction. The mating call. For it had been decided centuries ago, that this man would be the only one she would ever become intimate with. Her goddesses, his ancestors and some twist of fate had tied their destinies together. But it was always meant to end in death.

Such was the outcome of a Heretic and Puritan when they physically came together. It would unleash a curse so dark and powerful, no amount of love could withstand it. And here...between this human and her, there was absolutely no love at all. Just a burning hatred on her end which consumed her, and detachment on his part.

It didn't matter. Her body still throbbed for him like it always had. And she was determined to have her way with him, use him for her pleasure to satisfy her overpowering sexual urge just like he had done with her. And then...she was going to kill him.

She opened her mouth and let out another loud call as the waves crashed around her and the cold wind bit at her skin, sand clinging to her scales and hair. It was a call to her siren sisters, who waited deep inside the cave in the pool she resided in. To come and collect their prizes as well. She could see Raiz's two friends washed up on shore a little further. Her sisters would enjoy them while she took this one.

Her nether regions tingled at the very thought of mating with him at last. She hated the idea with all her soul, but her body perversely craved it. He had to be hers. All of him had to be hers. She would own him, dominate him and use him as much as she wanted before exacting her revenge. Before she gave him exactly what a cruel man like him deserved for breaking a vulnerable, young woman's heart without a second thought. A woman who had loved him with everything she had, risked it all for him. He would pay for his crimes tonight. It was finally time to put an end to his worthless existence.

Chapter 12

The Heretic

I woke up to the sound of water splashing all around me and the movement of something heavy and slippery on top of me.

"Fucking hell!" I cursed, trying to shift away from the creature which had me trapped inside a bathtub as it thrashed and grinded against me.

Horror seized me at the sight and feel of it as my brain registered what was happening. It...it was a... It was half fish and half woman...and its face was...hideous. Razor-sharp teeth, slanted eyes, gills on its neck...

I had never seen anything so ugly in my life.

"Hello, lover," the creature crooned at me, revealing those sharp teeth even more as it opened its mouth in a grin. "It's been a while."

I sucked in a breath at that voice... A voice which was unmistakably human and familiar. Peering into the creature's face, I calmed my breathing and managed to croak out a single name.

"Raya?"

She grinned at me even more, flipping her hair aside and sliding further up my body until our faces were so close, her breath mixing with mine, her salty scent starting to surround me, her slippery, scaly tail pinning my lower body under the water. I was in some sort of dark cave and the bathtub was made up of smooth shells and pearly stone, providing illumination for us because it emanated this ethereal glow.

"You remember me," she said in a huskier tone this time, one sharp-nailed finger tracing the line of my jaw.

It was hard to keep staring into her eyes. They spoke of death and horror. Dark promises of pain, misery and doom. And the ugliness of her features made me very uncomfortable. But I didn't look away. I had a feeling she would not like that...might respond very...viciously.

"What happened to you?" I asked her in a whisper, frowning deeply. "How did you...turn into this?"

She smoothed her red hair away from her face so that her features were even more visible and prominent, inciting no small amount of fear in me. I may be the Heretic who was feared across the seas in this part of the world, but in that moment, I wasn't feeling too brave or cutthroat. I was up against something I had never before encountered. I had no crew. No weapons. And...I was unclothed.

She ran her tongue along the seam of her darkened lips as she noted the expression on my face. "I do not owe you answers to such questions, Heretic," she hissed at me, placing both her hands on my shoulders. "You are only here to do my bidding. To pleasure me. To mate with me. And then, you will be given back to the ocean."

Mate? What the hell was she talking about? There was no chance of me ever sleeping with a creature as ugly and terrible as this. I felt myself getting a little angry then. She couldn't have me when she was pretty and desirable. What made her think she could have me now when no man on this earth would even consider...?

Raya suddenly opened her mouth and began to sing, interrupting my thoughts. And at the sound of her melodious voice, I felt all my good sense leaving me. Damn. It was the same song I had heard in my desperate race to the shore. I wasn't sure how much time had passed since then, but I found myself not even caring anymore.

"You're beautiful," I whispered, staring at her and feeling like I needed her to breathe.

Raya smiled as she sang that haunting tune, caressing my shoulders the whole time. "Mmm. I really am, aren't I?" she said before continuing her singing.

Yes. She really was. I don't know how come I had thought she was ugly or that I had anything to fear from her. She was everything. A goddess of the ocean. Made for me. Her song was just for me. She needed me to take her ache away. And I was more than eager to do so.

I let out a groan when she trailed her sharp claws down my torso and then gripped my aching cock, rubbing the tip of it along her crotch. The friction aroused me even more as I surrendered to her administrations and let her fill herself up with my erection.

I was hers to do what she wished with me now...

Chapter 13

Raiz

200 years. It has been 200 fucking years. And I still remember how she killed me. How she fucked me in her siren form while I was half drunk on her allure. How she tore at my neck with her savage teeth, ripped into my chest with her claws, over and over as I gasped for air and tried to beg her for mercy. Blood had spurted everywhere, the water in that tub going red within seconds, her horrendous face splattered with it as she grinned at me cruelly. My cock had still been inside her, limp and useless. And she took so much pleasure in destroying what little life had been left in me after all her torture.

Sirens were cruel, brutal creatures. There was no mercy in them. They hated men. They reveled in the destruction of those too weak to resist them. They used and killed. It was in their mechanism. It was what all the legends told. And yet every seaman in history was vulnerable to the danger they presented.

Me? I wasn't just vulnerable. I was fated to die at her hands. No matter how many lifetimes I lived, no matter how many times I was born, my death was written at the hands of a siren. Deep down, I had always carried the knowledge of my ancestors in my soul ever since Ayran and what had happened to me back then. What had happened to my friends who had bound themselves to me and as a result, bound themselves to the curse as well. Tamar and Kal. We weren't brothers by blood. We'd grown up together on the streets and had amassed an empire, determined to succeed as brothers. And we *had* succeeded.

But a few feet away in that cabin I had just left, my death awaited me. It was a sure thing. She might claim to love me, but that could also be her way to lure me to my end. How could she love me after the way we had been living all this time? How could any woman love me? I had made sure that no one would. No love. No betrayal. No heartbreak. No curse.

I stared out at the water surrounding my yacht, the deck now starting to go quiet as many of my guests retreated into their cabins. I should go look for some headphones. Before she started singing, and I could no longer remain in control of my senses. At least I could try to be smarter this time. Try to protect myself and my brothers. She could hurt them too. I planned to do everything in my power to prevent that from happening.

'Not tonight, Siren,' I muttered, shaking my head at the dark ocean and then walking back to my cabin.

Juliet was my enemy, yeah, but I still wanted to make sure she was fine. She genuinely did not seem to have any clue as to what she was or who I really was. That near-death episode she'd had in the tub seemed to have triggered something locked deep within her, brought her true visage to the forefront. But she hadn't looked murderous afterwards. She'd just seemed scared.

Don't fall for it, Raiz. She could be pretending.

Maybe...just like the Raya in my past, her powers had been lying dormant and were now unleashed. Maybe her seeing me in the arms of another woman tonight had sent her hurtling inside that part of herself she never touched. I hadn't known that my wife was in love with me all this time. She did a great job at pretending she couldn't stand me.

And that in itself should warn me. How great she was at pretending. I needed to be careful. I couldn't allow myself to trust her or fall for her wiles. It wasn't safe or smart.

I found her asleep, curled up in bed, and was relieved to see that her legs were back. Thank the Gods. She was scary in her monstrous form. So fucking scary. I swallowed again when I remembered the way she had killed me, those memories and that pain still so vivid in my mind. She was a vicious, vengeful creature whom I needed to steer clear of.

Carefully, I opened the bedside drawer and retrieved my earphones. I hoped this worked. Damned inconvenient to sleep with these things plugged in, but my life was on the line here. I couldn't let history repeat itself. There had to be some kind of a solution to this. Jesus. *Fuck*. I was stressed out of my mind.

I observed that in her sleep, Juliet appeared very small and helpless, but I wasn't fooled. I clenched my jaw as I studied her, wearing those cream silk PJs I had bought for her last month. She didn't know that it was chosen by me. My secretary had had some stuff delivered to the house during her birthday party and that was part of it, along with some other gifts from me. I hadn't told her any of it was from me. And I never questioned myself as to why I insisted on personally buying every present for my wife.

My wife.

God, I'd ended up marrying her! How could I have known? She didn't look anything like Raya. She didn't behave like her either. She wasn't demanding or ravenous during sex. When I felt myself desiring her so much that I couldn't hold back, she would mostly lie there and barely respond to me. It was humiliating to go through that as a man. So I stopped fucking her. I fucked other girls instead who didn't make me feel like I wasn't wanted.

With a frown, I raised the coverlet on the bed and gently draped it over her. She appeared cold. God, why the fuck did I even care? I should be planning her death right now.

Shaking my head, I straightened and was about to leave when I heard her say my name. I froze, wondering how I was going to shut out her voice if she started to sing to me right now. There was no music because I'd left my phone in the other cabin.

"I'm sorry I fucked your brother, Raiz," Juliet mumbled, making me glance at her in surprise.

Her eyes were still closed. She seemed to be talking in her sleep. But I heard her very clearly.

"I don't want to be that kind of woman. He was good, but I love you. Please don't give up on me."

The only thing my brain could focus on was 'I fucked your brother' and ' He was good'.

I was going to fucking kill him.

I couldn't believe this. Him putting his dirty hands on her. That son of a bitch. He was supposed to have my back.

I barely remembered crossing the passageway to get to his room, finding him standing near the open glass doors of his cabin which led out on to the deck. It wouldn't have mattered if he had been asleep. I would have dragged his ass out of bed and beaten the shit out of him while he was still half asleep.

Tamar turned only just in time for me to land a hard punch to his jaw, sending him thudding against the doors behind him, his glass of whatever he'd been drinking falling to the floor.

"You fucking bastard," I shouted as I pulled him back up and readied myself to punch his face again. "She's my wife, you motherfucker!"

Tamar dodged me easily this time, shoving me back and ducking out of my range as I whirled to glare at him, my breaths coming out hard and fast.

"Technically, it is wife-fucker," he had the audacity to throw in my face. "Or maybe sister-in-law- fucker-"

"Shut the hell up!" I roared at him. "Do you want me to kill you?"

He raised his eyebrows at me, looking me up and down like he'd never seen me before.

"Wow," he finally breathed while I struggled not to launch myself at him and hurt him till I saw some blood.

"You know...if you put half as much effort into your marriage as you're putting in punishing me for sleeping with her, this wouldn't have happened in the first place," he stated, rubbing his jaw. "Look at you. You look like a madman. Is this purely territorial or are you genuinely feeling betrayed by me right now. I thought you didn't give a fuck about her."

I stared at him mutinously until he stopped that grin on his face from spreading any further and gulped, stepping further away from me.

"Seriously, brother? You're that bothered by it? Why? I don't understand."

I didn't understand either. I just stood there and knew in my bones that if he hadn't been my brother, I would have killed him right now. For touching her. What the hell was happening tonight? It was as if everything was shuffled around until my emotions were all over the place, and I was left feeling raw and exposed. Taken by surprise from all directions.

How could I care about a woman like that? Moreover, how could I make any of them remember that other life? It seemed that I was the only one cursed to live with those memories. My brothers had been shredded into pieces as well, screaming and drowning in their blood at the hands of those sirens. How could I put any of that aside and feel this kind of rage at the thought of her betraying me like this? Especially when I myself had being going around being faithless like I was on a fucking mission.

"I'm sorry," Tamar said, frowning at me in concern. "Listen, I didn't think you would care. That it would matter to you. She told me she was going to leave you. She's made up her mind, Raiz. She's grown tired of the way you treat her."

"I fucking know that," I growled at him, turning away and trying to calm down.

I should just let her go. It was for the best. The further away she was from me, the better. Maybe I could live out decades without dying at the hands of the woman I had once betrayed. Betrayed so cruelly that she'd chosen to embrace becoming a monster for life just so that she could end mine. A woman I hadn't been able to love and respect when she needed me so much. But one I had grown to love at last without even being aware of it all this time. I didn't want her to leave me. But letting her stay would be worse.

...

Chapter 14

The last thing Juliet expected to find as she exited the mall late one Saturday afternoon was her ex husband leaning against his car with his arms folded across that broad chest, sunglasses on, dressed in casual attire which consisted of a white shirt and jeans. Like waiting for her to join him after she was done with her shopping was the most natural thing in the world. She paused on the steps outside, regarding him uncertainly, trying to ignore the painful feeling in her heart at the sight of him after so long. It had been over a year since their divorce. He'd let her leave peacefully, even giving her a good amount of money to get started on her new life instead of leaving her destitute like he could have.

She'd found a job working as an assistant, trying to keep a low profile after their very public separation. She stalked his social media like a pathetic ex and then later chastised herself for it because he was always with some other girl. Hating Raiz had become impossible for her after she had admitted how she truly felt for him that night. That last night on the yacht during his party.

She still shuddered when she thought of it. She'd begun therapy because of it, but there were still so many questions left unanswered in her mind. Raiz had the answers. Juliet knew he did. But he'd wanted nothing to do with her, and she didn't try to push him to talk.

But seeing him now, right here in front of her, it made her weak all over again. Shit. What was the matter with her? Any self-respecting female would simply put her chin up and walk away. Ignore the hell out of him. But she found herself being pulled towards him like a moth to the flame, stopping again when they were only several inches apart.

"Juliet," he murmured, finally removing his glasses.

Looking into his dark, penetrating gaze made her heart flutter even more.

"Hey," she said breathlessly. "What're you doing here?"

Raiz glanced down at the bags she was holding, surprising her when he took them and placed them in the backseat of his car before turning back to her.

"Let me give you a ride," he said with a faint smile, opening the passenger door and waiting for her to get in.

She swallowed nervously as she looked up at his tall frame, torn between her integrity and the fact that her heart was beating so fucking fast just from the excitement of being so close to him again and having his attention on her. She was curious and very much eager to get in the car with him.

Not taking her eyes off his ruggedly handsome features, Juliet climbed in as he held the door open, giving her a smirk before going over to the driver's side once she was settled.

"Where are you taking me?" she asked him, her heart pounding faster than it had in over a year.

Raiz removed his glasses to give her a possessive look, his expression strong and determined. "Where you belong, Juliet. I'm taking you home with me."

She breathed in sharply and looked away, butterflies in her stomach, an ache between her legs and her heart squeezing from emotions. He'd come for her. She couldn't believe that he wanted her back. That he hadn't been able to forget her either.

Chapter 15

Raiz
I didn't bother with any foreplay. It wasn't the time to linger and take note of details. I just wanted some raw, lustful sex, and so I told her to strip and get on the bed.

She got the message loud and clear, wasting no time as she let her clothes drop to the floor and spread out for me. For me. It was all for me. After all this time, Juliet still wanted me. Standing at the foot of the bed, I studied the pink tipped breasts she was already rubbing, her thighs parted, the center of which was glistening with moisture.

Bending my head, I bent to give it a long lick, realizing just how wet and swollen she already was. Good. I liked doing the work most of the time, but right now, I was just too horny and frustrated.

Unzipping myself, I let my cock out and gave it a few strokes while watching her writhing and sighing in anticipation. I was hard as a nut within seconds and placed one knee on the bed while asking her to put a pillow under her back.

When she was in position, I slid my cock inside her cunt and groaned at the intense sensation of burying my dick inside her while her pussy gripped me. Fuck, yes.

It was over within a minute. Neither of us could make it last. Neither of us wanted to.

...

Juliet stood near the window, sunlight sparkling in her hair, the lines and curves of her figure looking even more appealing in the thin, white shirt she wore. After a thorough fuck fest all last night, I was more than a little exhausted, but Juliet did not seem to be having that problem. She sipped her coffee in silence while looking outside at the rising dawn, and I looked my fill at her, the sensation of my cock stirring surprising me a little. But then, not so surprising because she never failed to get me going no matter the time of the day or night. No matter how tired I was, or how busy, all she had to do was look at me invitingly, and I melted.

"Baby," I grumbled from the bed, needing her back in my arms again.

I couldn't stay without her for too long these days.

She turned to me and gave me a smile, leaning back against the window pane, a cup of coffee in her hands.

"Good morning, my love."

I became a simp for her whenever she called me that. After I'd brought her back home a few weeks ago, I did everything in my power to convince her that I could be a good husband. I didn't care about the curse anymore. I wanted my wife. I wanted us to make it this time. Make this relationship work against all odds. Juliet was mine. She had always been destined for me. And this time, it was not going to result in pain and destruction. It would be for our happiness. I'd do anything.

I was so tired of feeling nothing. Tired of this cold bastard I had become. It was time to let go and show her that I was not the enemy. In another lifetime I had hated her, tried to run from her, avoided her. Maybe that was why it had ended badly. This lifetime will be different. I was going to learn how to love her the way she deserved.

"How long have you been up?" I asked with a smile, throwing my legs over the side of the bed and sitting up before stretching.

Juliet walked over to me, putting her coffee aside and holding out a hand. "Long enough to start missing you like crazy. Swim?"

I glanced outside the French doors to our pool in the back patio. It looked very inviting this morning, and I always enjoyed a fresh dip in it every morning.

Getting to my feet, I picked her up in my arms, grinning at the delighted sound she made. My sexy as hell wife. The love of my life. Walking outside with her like that, I counted to three to prepare her before tossing her inside the warm water which was waiting for us. I was diving in after her before her head even broke the surface and she came up for air.

"I love you," she said to me, twining her arms and legs around me and giving me a long kiss.

I loved her too. So much that I couldn't imagine the thought of losing her anymore. I wasn't gonna fuck it up this time.

As tempted as I felt to continue the kiss and maybe let it lead to something else, I gently released her and decided to do a few laps as part of my workout routine. There will be time for sex later.

I had a business meeting to attend at around ten, and then nothing else for the rest of the day. It would be a good idea to plan something with Juliet and take her out later this evening.

Later on, I rested my forearms on the concrete, trying to catch my breath while looking out at the ocean beyond our infinity pool. Something was bothering me, and I knew it had a lot to do with the text I had received last night. From Catherine, the girl I'd been sleeping with on occasion last year. She'd said something about meeting up, and I'd been half asleep when I'd received her message, so I hadn't responded. She had no idea that I was back with my wife, but I still needed to start setting some very strict boundaries with the women from my past. Things were different now. I didn't want to hurt Juliet anymore.

"The ocean looks so beautiful." She came up from behind me and wrapped her arms around my torso, resting her chin on my shoulder as we looked out at the horizon together.

I felt peace for the first time in years and turned my head to kiss her temple, frowning at the intensity of my feelings for her. I could feel. I really could feel so deeply. I just needed to believe in love. Believe in us.

"Full of hope, isn't it?" I murmured, turning my attention back to the sea with a relaxed sigh. "Hope. Love. And new beginnings, Juliet. I'll make it right this time."

She caressed my shoulders and biceps slowly, her body languidly moving against mine in the water, and I felt myself getting hard.

"I want you," I whispered to her, twisting around so I could kiss her properly.

But my breath jammed in my throat when I saw what she was morphing into, the way she stared at me as she changed, vengeance burning so clearly in her eyes.

"Juliet," I said, shaking my head at her. "No. No, please, don't do this. I love you."

She grinned at my words, the sharp teeth becoming visible now. "You love me?" she mocked. "Did you tell Catherine that? Or were you planning on continuing to fuck other women as much as possible while still trying to keep me?"

"What? No. I was going to tell her-"

"Lies!" she spat at me and with one vicious swipe of her claw, she cut me across the face.

I let out a sharp cry of pain, slapping my hands to my cheek as blood spurted out of my wound.

"Juliet, listen to me-" I moaned, trying to speak through the pain.

"No. You listen to me, Raiz Al' Ahmid," she grated out, pinning me back against the concrete with her heavy tail and supernatural strength. "Listen good for it is the last thing you will be hearing in this lifetime. My love."

Then she started to sing, and for a few seconds, while my senses were still working fine, I felt the pain and loss so acutely. Tears trickled down my cheeks, stinging the wound across my face which was bleeding so much.

"Raya...." I whispered sadly. "Forgive me."

I sensed only a moment of hesitation in her before her gaze hardened and she raised the pitch of her voice slightly, sending me into a hypnosis which would once again, lead to my death at the hands of the woman I had scorned centuries ago. She would mate with me again, and then kill me. Again.

It was fated. Why did I let myself think this time would be any different?

Chapter 16

She stared numbly at his floating corpse, surrounded by a mix of red and blue. He was gone again. And it was for the best. She didn't care how many lifetimes she lived with this man, she would find him in every one and end him.

Except she had had second thoughts this time around. When he'd uttered those last words...there had been something in his gaze. Not horror, fear or disgust. But genuine remorse. Slowly, Juliet felt herself reverting to her human form, still looking at Raiz's body with a blank expression.

During the few weeks she'd been here, back in his life, she had kept having strange dreams, flashbacks of an existence long ago, repeated words of some ancient curse. Then she'd read the message from Catherine on his phone last night and it had triggered her, making her believe that this man was capable of one thing and one thing only. Betrayal.

These few weeks had become unreal to her then. Had seemed like lies he fed her for reasons she could not fathom. All she could picture was him cheating on her again,. Making a fool of her again.

She had been in the shower early that morning when every realization, every suppressed memory had hit her with the blast of the water over her exhausted body. Their shared history, who they really were and what their destiny was. She'd felt nothing but hatred for him in that moment, wanting nothing but revenge. To destroy him as she was meant to do so.

So why wasn't she satisfied this time?

Juliet swallowed the lump of pain in her throat as a barrage of doubts flooded her mind. What if she had been mistaken this time? What if he had been sincere? She had never seen Raiz look at her like he did during those last moments, with resignation and regret but also so much love. Had he loved her after all? Had this lifetime managed to give them something they had not been able to attain before?

Juliet reached for his lifeless form, running her now human hands over the wounds she had slashed across his body, beginning to cry silently at the hopelessness of it all. She'd killed him despite having experienced that inkling of doubt about doing so. And now he was gone. And her soul was empty again.

"I love you," Juliet whispered, putting her cheek against his shoulder. "I always loved you. Only you."

She cradled his face in her hands. A face which was hardly even recognizable thanks to her viciousness. Kissing the shredded flesh of his bloody lips, she cried hard, regret seizing her in that instant, her mind filled with images of the two of them together these past few weeks, the bliss she had experienced in his arms, all the broken things she thought they had fixed between them.

She had let her hatred consume her so much that she put more faith in that curse instead of being brave enough to give this love a fighting chance.

"Forgive me too, Raiz," she said, closing her eyes and not letting him go as the bleakness of her existence bore down on her.

MAYBE...THE NEXT LIFETIME would be different. Maybe some day, their love would be more powerful than this curse. She lifted her head with renewed determination, knowing what she had to do for the rest of this life she had. She would travel every corner of this earth and leave a clue for herself to find no matter where she was born next. She would fill up the corners of this world with memories of her pain and love, so that when she was reborn, she would know what mistakes not to repeat. She would remind herself and him of their history before it was too late. And together, they would fight this. One day, they could truly belong to each other, and find a way to be happy.

...

Song: Evanescence : My Immortal

About The Author

ANA STORM is the M/F romance penname 0f author Z. S. STORM who mostly writes dark fiction, romance and fantasy books.

You can connect with him on Goodreads or email him at: z.s.storm.author@gmail.com

Link to newsletter and other platforms: https://linktr.ee/zsstorm

Don't miss out!

Visit the website below and you can sign up to receive emails whenever ANA STORM publishes a new book. There's no charge and no obligation.

https://books2read.com/r/B-A-FXHMC-HCOTC

BOOKS 2 READ

Connecting independent readers to independent writers.

Also by ANA STORM

Dreamhaven Duet
The Stable Boy

Standalone
Dirty Secrets
Girl Obsessed
Maybe Someday
Ride Or Die : A 'Girl Obsessed' novella
Girl Obsessed
Ex Habit
Girl Obsessed